Copyright © 2022 by Leslie Isaacs
ISBN 9798831571561
Independently Published
All rights reserved.
Published in the United States by KDP.

Special Thanks and Dedication

To my precious little children,
Thank you for all your questions after I told you the first story of Harry.
Because of your imagination and curiosity, the other stories were born.
To my husband Gregory,
I did it again! Thank you for your support and believing in me.

To Jason Sturgill,
Thank you for bringing Harry to life through picture so that children all
over the world can see what I see.
To Metasha Rader,
Thank you for your expertise on editing and English skills.
To Melissa Hembree Isaacs,
You mean more to me than you know. You helped shine the light on the path to my
illustrator when I was stuck and didn't know where to go.

To all my supporters and fans,
This second book wouldn't have come out without you telling me how much you
loved Harry's first book.
To all the children that this book will reach know these things:
You can do anything if you set your mind to it.
You should never judge people just by what's on the outside.
You can have friends who don't like the same things as you.

With a full heart and so much love, Thank you ALL!

Harry the Dragon and the Bake Sale

Visit our website
www.HarryTheDragon.com
for upcoming events, information on new books being published and merchandise.
We also go to schools
for book readings.
Go to our website and email us to schedule your school.

lived a friendly dragon named Harry.

Harry was always volunteering around in town with whatever needed to be done.
He helped replace a roof on Mrs. Jenkins' house when a strong storm blew the shingles off.
He piled up branches after the heavy ice storm came last winter, and trees fell all over the town.
He helped whenever and wherever he was needed.

He received a letter in the mail one day from the town's school saying they were having a
BAKE SALE FUNDRAISER for the Reading Program if anyone would like to volunteer.

Harry immediately was thrilled to help the school and bake his favorite food – cornbread.

Finally, the day arrived for the bake sale. He gathered all his supplies and started baking early that morning. Soon, he had several pans— or as Harry called them "pones"— of cornbread ready, and off he headed to the school.

He started setting up his table like most of the other volunteers and waited for the customers to stop by.

He knew most everyone in town now after he had been welcomed by the townspeople following everyone finding out that he didn't eat people. People came and went buying his famous cornbread to help with the School Fundraising.

But then he saw someone he had never seen before. She was the most beautiful dragon he had ever seen!

She came to his table to see what he had made. Harry stood there for a moment and then finally was able to speak to her.

"Hello. Would you like some cornbread?" Harry asked, swooning over her.
"No, thank you. I don't like cornbread," she replied.

"YOU DON'T LIKE CORNBREAD?!?!?"
Harry was flabbergasted!!
How could someone NOT like cornbread?!?!?!

"No, I don't. But thank you just the same. My name is Ella. I have a table down the hall with my baked goods," she said smiling.

"Nice to meet you, Ella.
My name is Harry," Harry smiled.
Ella walked on down the hall to see what the other volunteers had brought.
Harry watched Ella walking away until he got another customer.

When he looked back up, he couldn't see her. His heart flipped and flopped scared that he would never see her again! He must go find her table!

Ella's table was only 7 tables down from Harry's table when he found her! "Well, hello again!" Ella said grinning.

"Hello again!" Harry said smiling.

"What have you made for today?"
"Grandma's Gritty Fudge," Ella announced, offering Harry a piece.

"NO, THANK YOU!" Harry replied with his nose in the air and his face turning green. "I DON'T LIKE FUDGE!!!!"
"You don't like fudge?!"
Ella looked shocked. Fudge was her favorite food. She loved fudge as much as Harry loved his cornbread.

"Nope. I hope that's ok?" Harry was a little worried thinking that maybe Ella wouldn't talk to him anymore.
But Ella smiled at Harry and said, "That's ok. Different people like different foods. Or in our case different DRAGONS like different FOODS." They both laughed and smiled at each other.

Harry blurted out, "Would you like to go get some hot chocolate at the coffee shop in town tomorrow morning?!"

Eeeeeeeeekkkkk!! What had Harry just said!? What would Ella say?!?!

"Hot cocoa is my second favorite food! I would love to!"

The next morning Harry met Ella at the coffee shop in town. They talked and talked about the fundraiser and what a success it was. The school had raised $2,000 with the help of all the volunteers in town. That money would provide the extra help needed for so many children with their reading. After 2 hours of visiting and drinking hot cocoa, Harry asked Ella if she would like to go eat supper with him that night.

"Do you like Italian food?" Harry asked nervously wondering what Ella would say. "I love it!" Ella replied.

"My cousin Leonardo owns the Italian restaurant here in town. Would you like to have dinner there tonight with me?" Harry loved spaghetti almost as much as he loved cornbread but not quite as much.

"I could think of nothing I would love better than to have dinner with you." Ella smiled.

They met that evening and Cousin Leonardo fixed them a lovely meal. Spaghetti stacked high with meatballs, fettuccini, lasagna, and a delicious garlic bread.

Cousin Leonardo came over to see Harry and his new friend Ella.

"I hope you have enjoyed your meal. Cooking Italian food and feeding people has been my dream job since I was a child. Thanks to Harry, the townspeople now know we dragons don't eat people but love all kinds of good food. I am so very proud of my restaurant," Cousin Leonardo told them.

"It was the best food that I have had in a long time! Thank you so much," Ella replied.

"You are welcome and thank you, Miss Ella! My cousin Harry looks happy tonight being here with you," said Cousin Leonardo.

Harry thanked Cousin Leonardo for the meal and paid the bill.

Ella and Harry walked through the town of Kay-Ma-Zoo that evening.

They stopped and sat at the fountain in the middle of town. They talked about what a lovely dinner they had. "Would you like to eat with me again sometime?" Harry asked, hoping Ella would say yes. This had been the best day of his life."I would love to...
but... only if we come back to Cousin Leonardo's," Ella laughingly glanced at Harry. Harry agreed without a moment's thought.

From then on, every day they would have hot cocoa of a morning at the coffee shop in town, and every night they would eat supper at Cousin Leonardo's Italian Restaurant.

This went on for the whole summer.

One evening after supper when they were walking down the street in Kay-Ma-Zoo, they stopped by the fountain in the middle of the town square. This is where they had stopped that first evening and had talked about the best day that they had ever had. Harry had been planning to stop here at the fountain for a couple of weeks now.

He had this all planned out. He had gone to his Aunt June's jewelry shop and picked out the most beautiful ring!

There was a band playing in the gazebo close by. The fountain was lovely.

"YES!!!!" Ella squealed out!
Harry smiled with joy in his eyes, "Now, it's time to plan for the wedding!"
"And to think all of this came from us volunteering for the Bake Sale at the School!" Ella was so thrilled.
"I think I know of two foods that MUST be at the reception! Cornbread and Gritty Fudge!" Harry said.
"That sounds like a lovely start to the menu already!" Ella smiled.

31

THE END
(FOR NOW)

Ella's Gritty Fudge Recipe
From Leslie's Mamaw Carrie's Kitchen

3 Cups sugar
2 TBS cocoa
Dash of salt
1 Cup milk

Mix ingredients together in the pot.
Boil until soft ball or 240°
Remove from heat.

Then add:
1 tsp vanilla
1 stick butter
Stir until it starts to fudge.

Place in dish and let harden. As it cools the top will begin to have light spots appear. This will allow you to know that it's cooling and almost ready to cut and enjoy. You will have delicious GRITTY FUDGE.

How many hidden hearts can you find in this book?

Go to www.HarryTheDragon.com for the answer.

Made in the USA
Monee, IL
30 September 2022

14375915R00021